The Adventure of The Missing Partner

James Michael Borden

Published by NorthForest Books

Print ISBN: 979-8-9878806-9-2
eBook ISBN: 979-8-9878806-0-9

Printed in the United States of America
Revised Edition

Contents

Part One

1. Call to a Primitive Land — 7
2. Monday, December 12, 1892 — 14
3. Tuesday, December 13, 1892 — 29

Part Two

4. Death, Deception, and Dogsleds — 39
5. Wednesday, December 14, 1892 — 42
6. Thursday, December 15, 1892 — 47
7. Friday, December 16, 1892 — 51
8. Saturday, December 17, 1892 — 64
9. Sunday, December 18, 1892 — 68
10. Monday, December 19, 1892 — 70
11. Tuesday, December 20, 1892 — 71

Afterword — 75
Acknowledgments — 77

Part One

Call to a Primitive Land

The regular consumer of my accounts would know that after *The Adventure of the Final Problem* (published in 1891), I reported, based on the evidence gathered at Reichenbach Falls, which included a farewell letter written in the hand of Sherlock Holmes, that he was gone forever. He had taken that nemesis of humanity, Professor Moriarty, over the precipice with him. For the turn my life has taken since, they might as well have brought me over the edge with them.

I had been mourning the death of Holmes for the better part of a year. To make matters worse, my medical practice had been tortuously slow.

In early November of 1892, a rapid knock came upon my consulting room door. I opened it and was met by the bent-over visage of a grizzled sailor wearing his oilers and cap.

"May I be of some service?" I began.

He closed the door and began speaking in a voice I knew intimately but somehow did not belong to the person in front of me. He undid his outer garments, false sideburns, and a

7

mustache as he spoke, straightening into the personage of Mr. Sherlock Holmes. For the shock, I can't recall what he said, only his tone of voice: It was as mundane as when we two were seated in front of a crackling fire at 221 B Baker Street any number of times before his disappearance over Reichenbach Falls the previous year.

"Sorry to give you such a start, old bean. More than any other person, I have regretted any anguish I may have caused by letting you believe I was deceased. There was a mortal struggle between myself and the diabolical Moriarty. But for a well-timed jiu-jitsu throw, I, rather than he, would have met death in the chasm. Unfortunately, Moriarty had brought a confederate with him on that day who, upon seeing the demise of his boss, took it upon himself to finish the job by rolling a few boulders down on me. The scoundrel probably never knew if I had been killed, but the gang at large would probably hold out the possibility that I could live to undo their evil deeds. For the necessity of survival, not only from the remnants of the Moriarty gang but also from lesser criminal associations, I needed the world to believe I was deceased," said he. The meaning of his words began to penetrate my consciousness. Yet, while I accepted them as truth, it was hours before I could rise above a torrent of emotion and welcome my companion back into my life. Holmes would first endure some untoward curses for letting me believe he had died. What little effort would it have taken to curtail my state of perpetual mourning? Still, in the end, I realized that as I had endured his inconsideration and shortcomings innumerable times in the past, I would yet again. It would be useless to waste any effort rebuking Sherlock Holmes for being who he is. Besides, he had already launched an extraordinary proposition: "Watson, I have concluded that I can best serve the civilized world by continuing my investigations under the cloak of anonymity. I also feel it beneficial to extend my absence, so I would like to request the greatest favour I ever have asked over our many years of friendship."

"What could that be, Holmes?"

"I have decided that I need to take an extended journey away from here—to put a great physical distance between myself and England—so that I may, unimpeded, take up my native trade once more. My brother, Mycroft, has received inquiries from some prominent Americans who have found their lives entangled in crime. These clients are very wealthy; they will absorb any expense to remove these scourges from their lives. That is to say, Watson, if you can get permission from your lovely wife to take a sabbatical, I will share my considerable compensation with you! What do you say, old friend?"

Before I consented, I presented my wife with the proposal, perhaps too forcefully. She agreed, stating, "You should know what is best," but then she turned away. Despite our many cordial letters, this image haunted me the entire voyage.

I closed my business affairs and was ready to depart in five days. Our client had advanced a satchel of American currency and two passports. Our luggage preceded us to Victoria Station. We followed in a hansom cab, taking the Great London Railroad and Western Railroad to Liverpool, where we boarded the RMS *Majestic*. This massive steamship, driven by two screws, is the swiftest of the Star Line. We were furnished with two lavishly appointed first-class staterooms, as posh as any hotel in London or Paris. I had just finished unpacking my trunk when I heard the lonely blast of the ship's steam whistle overhead. We were already making headway toward the Atlantic Ocean. The seedy grey shipyards of Liverpool soon gave way to the purity of sea and sky.

The crossing to New York took nine days. Holmes said little. Except for our breakfasts and dinners, served en masse in the ship's elegant dining room, he remained in his cabin. That said, Holmes was quite cordial with fellow diners. He introduced himself as Winthrop Stevens without offering any personal information.

The Atlantic Ocean churned with storms the whole of our crossing. The sea was fascinating; I found myself clutching the rail of the outer deck, mesmerized by its power. However, too much time in the chilly air resulted in an aching from an old bullet wound—my souvenir from the Afghan campaign.

Despite the considerable speed of our crossing, it was a relief to set my feet on solid ground again. Our client sent his valet and a gilded carriage to greet us at New York Harbor. He waited there, holding a sign with the name Winthrop Stevens written across it as per instructions. Holmes winced at the ostentatious coach and reluctantly climbed in. We were whisked to an estate on the upper east side of Manhattan Island.

There, Sherlock Holmes unraveled a conspiracy that American history books will surely recount. I am not at liberty to divulge any details except that it involved the financing of railroads. While Holmes focused his unique powers on a resolution, I toured New York and witnessed the centrifugal energy of the New World. From that time forward, London, dear London, by contrast, would seem like an aging dynasty receding perpetually into the fog of history. I judged it best not to share these thoughts with Holmes.

Our New York client referred Holmes to another possible case in early December that came via his fellow railroad tycoons. It seems a founding partner of an iron-ore mining concern called B & W Mines had disappeared into the wilds of Minnesota without a trace. Iron ore is an essential ingredient in steel manufacturing in any burgeoning country. The necessity of the mineral and the prospect of panic gave several key bankers and investors the jitters. Our New York client recommended Holmes to these businessmen under the provision that they agreed to keep his identity a secret. I, in turn, promised I would not chronicle any future cases until Holmes either retired or felt it otherwise safe to do so.

A few telegrams later, we were engaged in our next adventure! The investors informed us they had also hired a top agent from the Pinkerton Agency. In addition to our fixed fees and expense reimbursements, they promised a $2000 reward to the investigator who produced an arrest and conviction, should foul play be involved. I knew from our experiences that Holmes preferred working independently. It would be imperative to get to the evidence before it was tampered with.

The journeys by train to Chicago and St. Paul were interminable. Upon arriving in St. Paul, we dined and slept a mere four hours before Holmes guided my weary body back to the station. We then boarded a train on the St. Paul and Duluth Railroad, heading due north. Getting to our final destination, Gunflint City, at this time of year would necessitate crossing a treacherous stretch of Lake Superior via a small steamer to Port Arthur, Canada. From there, we would ride the Port Arthur, Duluth and Western Railway (known as the PADW) for the final ninety-one-mile journey, crossing back into Minnesota and going uphill to Gunflint City.

As it turned out, our steamer was a 118-foot wood boat called the *Hiram R. Dixon*, owned by the Booth Company, which operates a herring fishery further up Lake Superior. It was late in the season, but the investors in B & W Mines paid them well to make the journey, with the two of us being the sole passengers. The captain was intimately familiar with the shoals on the north shore of the lake. Given that the sky was clear and in a waning gibbous moon phase, he agreed to make a night run. We chugged out of Duluth Harbor onto the icy lake. I made my way to a sleeping berth, where I found refuge from the cold under a pile of wool blankets. The gentle rhythm of the waves and the engine's drone lulled me to sleep. The following day, I woke up at six and went to the relatively warmer engine room for breakfast. Holmes was already there, looking rested.

Sometime before noon, we stopped at the Booth Fisheries on Isle Royale to pick up barrels of salted herring scheduled to be dropped off at Port Arthur. We reached Port Arthur by midafternoon. As arranged, the PADW locomotive and a few cars were idling nearby, awaiting our arrival. A few handshakes later, we had begun the final leg of our journey.

More an icebox than a train, it rattled miserably over snow-covered tracks for ten hours, empty save for the crew, Sherlock, and myself. A snowstorm had blown up, obliterating the view from the window, giving the sense that we were captive characters in a Jules Verne novel. It might have been a stimulating experience had I not been exhausted and nearly frozen. We finally arrived in Gunflint City at approximately 1 a.m. the following morning.

The seven-day journey had rattled my nerves and constitution. Of our arrival, I remember little more than the sensation of being physically spent. My depleted state must have contrasted sharply with Holmes' eager countenance and nervous energy. He locked his arm in mine, pulling me from the train and up the stairs into the Hotel de Marguerite. He deposited me on a bed, where I slept for eighteen hours.

Near dusk, I awoke to the mirthful chattering of several women on the floor beneath me. Their merriment mingled with the clinking of silverware and plates. The smell of cooked food wafted through the floorboards, reminding me I hadn't eaten in a day. Sitting up in bed, taking stock of our diminutive room, I wondered what had become of Holmes. As if by telepathy, a staccato knock came on the door, followed by my old friend. He sat on the corner of my bed, removing his pipe's long, black stem to speak.

"My dear Watson, in my haste to get here, I have neglected you terribly. Can you ever forgive me?"

The old soldier in me spoke, "There is nothing to forgive, Holmes; we needed to get here while the evidence was still fresh. I signed on for the trip, and by God, I will take my lumps."

"That's my old chum! You are too kind and astute as usual; making good headway was imperative. Much circumstantial evidence points to a crime motivated by greed here. Despite the handicap of arriving late after the missing partner's disappearance, I have developed some inferences, which I shall share with you. First, you will need some nourishment."

He gave a quick, sidelong smile. "I might as well make my next apology while we're alone: it seems like we've landed in a bevy of ill repute. Our proprietor, the enterprising Miss Marguerite Matthews, purveys more than hotel rooms."

I then understood the reason for the feminine presence in this squalid boom town. "Well, Holmes, let us pack up and find more honorable hospitality."

"I've anticipated your sentiments, Watson, but this is the only public hotel for fifty miles. I will, however, keep a keen eye out for our first opportunity to move. In the meanwhile, let us repair to the dining room; I understand Madame Marguerite takes her cooking seriously!"

Monday, December 12, 1892

The following morning, after breakfast, I stepped outside the hotel to view Gunflint City in the daylight. To call this mudhole a city was to exceed the limits of generosity. Although Madame's establishment was rustic, it had the closest resemblance to bona fide architecture in the town. Even so, the siding was unpainted. Rolled-out tarpaper was all that covered the roof boards. There was a score of other buildings: ramshackle living quarters, warehouses, and a small jail made of cobblestones and cement. The street consisted of frozen mud and tramped-down snow. The eye was led to large rock drilling rigs, no more than a stone's throw from the hotel. Dozens of men labored around one of these. They were underdressed for the freezing temperatures except for heavy gloves and boots, yet their intense exertion and muscular bodies seemed to keep them warm.

However, one thing was striking: Gunflint City was as homely as its environs were breathtaking. A vast forest of giant white and red pines overshadowed the little town. These trees had enough space between them to drive a team of horses through them. Here and there, a friendly patch of sunlight penetrated through the forest onto their massive trunks. The terrain was just as remarkable: a line of red and black rock outcrops cast deep shadows. They appeared as ancient faces gazing out onto the landscape.

Later that morning, Holmes threw open the door to our room, followed by two bearded men dressed in heavy fur garments, each carrying an armload of outdoor clothing.

"Drop them on the floor, gentlemen," Holmes instructed. "I will settle up with you by the day's end."

They looked me over without so much as a friendly nod and then proceeded out the door.

"Watson, we will soon be immersed in grueling weather. I took the liberty of outfitting us with a few authentic articles of fur trapper and native Ojibwe outerwear. They will keep us warm and fashionable in a backwoods way!"

Holmes arranged a separate pile for each of us and continued, "You may remember the old felted beaver top hats in fashion until the 1850s in London. The pelts came from this area and much of central Canada."

A fox-fur pillbox hat now replaced the deerstalker's hat I had seen on Holmes while sleuthing about in the London fog. He pulled it down over his ears and forehead. Then he slid into knee-high caribou-skin boots with the fur facing inside. These he called "mukluks." However, the piece de resistance was an elaborate cardinal-red blanket coat made of felted wool, interspersed with artful black stripes. Holmes slipped his hands through each armhole, pulling it on. There were no buttons to close the coat around the body. Holmes remedied this, selecting a wide, decorative belt from the pile on the floor and cinching it tight at the waist.

"Rather becoming, I fancy," he said with his grey eyes twinkling. I thought this self-compliment in earnest, for he regarded himself from several angles in the dresser mirror.

"It's your turn, Watson!"

My garb was identical, save that the color of the blanket coat was a deep blue with black edges and stripes. After donning it, I flipped the heavy hood over my head.

"Holmes, I believe this is the first time I've been warm since we arrived in Minnesota; I'm ready for anything now!"

"That is well, Watson. There is no time to squander; we have a midday appointment with the local sheriff and a Pinkerton detective at the jailhouse. By the way, we can temporarily dispense with my identity as Winthrop Stevens. My reputation hasn't penetrated the depths of this wilderness. Other than any public forum, I am ready to revert to my former self."

"I thank heaven, Holmes; your recent history has been surreal enough without my being able to call you by your given name!"

In a few minutes, we were standing inside the doorway of the Gunflint City jail, whose main room consisted of two barred cells on one side, a desk, and chairs on the other. Introductions were officiated by Sheriff Howard Bowman, a fit, lanky man with a droopy mustache and unkempt hair, both of which were in want of attention. His hands were disproportionately large and strong, as demonstrated by way of a firm, earnest handshake.

In contrast, the Pinkerton man was a handsome, well-kempt man with a neat mustache. On the table beside him was a blocked derby. He wore black woolen pants and a matching vest, out of which a gold chain draped from the buttonhole in his watch pocket. His outer coat bore small lapels that would have accentuated a bow tie, had he been wearing one. His affect, I thought, was incongruous with our surroundings. This manner of dress was more appropriate for the lobby of a theatre or gentleman's club than the rustic, workaday environment of Gunflint City. He rudely eyed our French Voyageur, swamp-dandy clothing. It was apparent that our relationship was off to a rocky beginning.

Though I was put off by him, I offered my hand. It was met with a limp handshake. All the while, his steely-blue eyes locked into those of my companion. He thrust his hand toward Holmes and spoke as if addressing a crowd.

"The name's Kingsley—Amos G. Kingsley. Pinkerton Agency."

"Sherlock Holmes. Delighted, I'm sure." Holmes picked up then dropped Kingsley's hand and pressed his fingers together abstractly.

"It seems that we are both in the employ of the same company, Mr. Kingsley. How do you propose that we work in tandem to bring this mystery to a speedy conclusion?"

"I've heard of your fame in England and am sure you rank at the top of your profession there, Mr. Holmes, but Pinkerton reigns first in *this* country, and for a good many reasons. You should know that our company prefers to share information only between *our* agents and, of course, designated public offi-cials. I promise to advise you on my general theories, but I won't have a lot of extra time at my disposal to report my every finding to you. I would suggest this: If one of us has a break-through, we share it but otherwise operate independently. If there are any arrests, Sheriff Bowman will make them. Do you find this arrangement agreeable?"

Holmes was circumspect in his reply, "Quite. Of course, I expect all uncovered evidence to be available for either party to inspect."

Sheriff Bowman broke in with a slow drawl through his drooping mustache, "Mr. Holmes, I have told Mr. Kingsley that would be the requirement." He tapped his hand on a heavy safe beside his desk. "We already have a few pieces of evidence presented by Mr. Kingsley here. You and Mr. Watson are also welcome to inspect them. Gentlemen, I will remind all three of you that I am the sole legal authority in this county, which means you will be subject to me. I don't care a fig what your mutual working arrangements are, but in the end, I will make the decisions on how to proceed."

I saw a visible change on the countenance of Sherlock Holmes—one that I recalled from our bachelor days rooming together on Baker Street in faraway London. On his furrowed brow was a hardened and peeved expression.

Holmes spoke, "I understand and agree most heartedly with your requirements, Sheriff Bowman. Now then, Mr. Kingsley, I would like to see what you have turned up thus far."

While the sheriff retrieved pertinent items from the safe, Kingsley assumed a lofty pose and began: "On Wednesday, November 28th, Karl Franz Weisner failed to show up at a scheduled meeting in Gunflint City with the financial backers in B & W Mines. His partner, Jon Bric, did not plan to attend as his purview in the partnership did not include banking arrangements. But Weisner didn't show up for the scheduled meeting, which was unusual because he prided himself on punctuality. The office manager dispatched a messenger to Weisner's cabin by way of dog sled. When the messenger arrived, he witnessed a most chaotic scene: a team of ten

Alaskan huskies harnessed to Weisner's dog sled with no sign of their master anywhere. The sled was lying on its side, heavily damaged, surely from being dragged through the woods without a musher. The messenger checked the entire premises but found no sign of Weisner. He unharnessed the team, fed them, and put them into their sheds, then mushed his way back to Gunflint City to raise the alarm."

Amos G. Kingsley looked down into his derby, tapped his fingers on the brim, and continued. "Some background is necessary here: By 1888, the partners had modest claims near Virginia, Minnesota, but the claim here in Gunflint City promised a mother lode, assuring their fortunes. Previously, they had been sharing a modest cabin on the south shore of Gunflint Lake, but now they could live in relative luxury. Weisner had a sumptuous cabin built for himself on the north shore of the lake. The same year Bric followed suit, building a new cabin next door to the original rustic cabin on the south shore. It should be noted that their company, B & W Mines, owns those three cabins. Gunflint Lake's only other white person is a cabin boy who serves both partners. His name is Devon Peters. He lived a short while in the original cabin in 1888, but soon the company built an additional structure exclusively for Devon on the south shore near Bric's place. The boy was tasked with several jobs serving both partners, including providing firewood, delivering provisions, and maintaining their respective dog teams. When I questioned the boy, he told me he had seen Weisner the day before his disappearance but that nothing seemed out of the ordinary."

Sheriff Bowman bent over and began turning the dial on the safe.

Kingsley continued his monologue. "I presume that it was from his own cabin that Weisner departed before he went missing; it is the only place other than Gunflint City where he kept provisions for his dogs. It is most likely that he was mushing his team toward his Gunflint City appointment when an accident or possibly foul play came upon him. It had been snowing hard that day and twice since, obliterating Weisner's trail. The mining company has employed the best trackers in the area over the last week, but they haven't found a trace of Weisner. Five days after he was reported missing, I arrived and began my investigation. Naturally, my first stop was Weisner's cabin, where I found some important evidence."

The sheriff, hearing his cue, pulled a handle down on a safe door that swung open, issuing a deep groaning sound. He reached inside and pulled out a piece of paper bearing the B & W Mines logo and three other documents.

Amos Kingsley never stopped to include the three of us in conversation but continued in a prosecutorial style that began to irritate me. He lifted out the sheet of paper with the B & W Mines moniker, setting it on the table in front of us. It was a note written in an unrefined, cursive script with spelling errors indicative of someone who seldom wrote and perhaps had a limited education. The letters were so large that the short note consumed most of the page. They read:

"I will take grate pleasure in killing you! Shister!!"

The note was unsigned. Kingsley placed another piece of paper on the table, also written in an identical cursive script. It was plain that the same hand had written them both. Kingsley pontificated:

"I'm sure you will agree these two documents betray the same handwriting. The second one is an interoffice memo written by none other than the dead miner's business partner, Jon Bric."

I let loose an audible "Oh, dear me" and looked to Holmes, but his countenance was as stony as the Great Sphinx of Giza. I began to think the ordeal Holmes and I had gone through to get here was for naught—that this mystery was a mundane crime, unworthy of his singular powers. Still, there was no telling from his expression whether he was angry, impatient, dubious, or accepting of the evidence laid out by this man.

Kingsley went on. "I found the threatening note and the two documents I'm about to show you inside a desk drawer in Weisner's cabin. The first document is a copy of the original partnership agreement, written in 1867. The relevant clauses are these: 1) Even though both partners put up the same amount in the initial investment, they split the net proceeds 60/40 in Weisner's favor. I would guess that this unequal split in the partners' profits was the grudge Mr. Bric was nursing when referring to Weisner as a "shyster." 2) There is a death clause that states, 'If one of the Partners meets an untimely death, in the absence of foul play, the surviving Partner will have rights to 100% of the deceased partner's profits, excepting any valid will to supersede this agreement.'"

Holmes gave a cursory inspection of each document. Kingsley continued, "The second document is an 1887 addendum to the partnership agreement to accommodate new investors in B & W Mines. The investors are two other bankers and a railroad company. 'The new investors will take 80% of the first profits from the mine until they have repaid their initial investments; thereafter, they will have rights to 50% of net profits in perpetuity.' You may have heard that this mine promises to produce a bonanza of iron ore. However, if gold and silver are discovered, the returns may be exponential."

Kingsley jabbed his finger in the air, adding, "This crisis could not have come at a more critical juncture. The partnership has not yet completed the mining infrastructure, nor has the mine produced any ore. The investors are already deeply concerned and could pull out of the deal if something threatened the tenets of the original claim. For this reason, we must practice the utmost discretion. Until we find Mr. Weisner dead or alive, the entire enterprise is in question."

Holmes set down the documents and lit a match to stoke his pipe. He took two quick puffs, assuring himself it was burning evenly, and began to speak: "Thank you, Mr. Kingsley, for your initial research and most interesting findings. I have made a few inquiries myself over the last day. For the time being, I feel it would be most profitable to concentrate my energy at Weisner's property and Gunflint Lake. I understand that all the cabins built are the property of B & W Mines. With the investors' permission and that of the remaining partner, Jon Bric, Watson, and I would like to stay in the original cabin on his property for a few days. Would the sheriff have any objections?"

The reply came, "Although that cabin has been vacant for a while, I'm sure the company can arrange for Devon to get it suitably comfortable."

Holmes gathered his outdoor clothing and turned to me. "Come, Watson, I would like to show you a unique mode of transportation!"

Holmes was outside the room and in the mud street before I could speak. I hurried behind him to the front of the Hotel de Marguerite, where two Native Americans stood by their sleds, each with ten dogs in harnesses.

"Watson, allow me to introduce you to Sakima, who will be one of our Ojibwe neighbors on Gunflint Lake. The other musher is his son, Animikii."

They both gave me a friendly nod but then reverted to a dignified silence. Holmes, as usual, had perceived what our necessities would be well before I even knew our next move. He had arranged with Madame Marguerite for two days of home-cooked meals to accompany us. We packed some clothing and personal items into rucksacks and left our unwieldy steamer trunks in the hotel. I took a sitting position near the rear of Animikii's sled, with my portion of the provisions tied to the sled frame. He stood behind me on the sled's thin runners, uttering a few syllables to the lead dog. The team strained at their harnesses, but the sled barely moved. The huskies were small, and perhaps the load, especially with my bulk, was too heavy for them. I felt a helpless embarrassment. But Animikii pushed the sled from the rear driver's handles, giving it enough forward momentum to start it in motion. I caught a glimpse of my old friend seated comfortably in Sakima's dog sled. They were already making headway down the slope that led to Gunflint Lake. I confess, I expected to be bounced and swayed into seasickness, but the ride on the deep cushion of snow was quite smooth.

Outfitted in my Voyageur's gear, I felt nearly native in the frozen landscape. I peered out of my blanketed coat hood, freeing my mind from this strange case. Animikii was quiet. With him behind me, I felt alone with the dogs—or perhaps a team member, sharing their comradery and wildness. (Oh, I wonder what London's Diogenes Club members would say of this!) At one point, we began to descend a steep hill. Animikii kept his hands on the sled handles and used the bottom half of his body in the snow to slow the sled down. I repressed an image in my mind of being dragged upside down in the event the sled capsized.

In a little less than an hour, we arrived at the shore of Gunflint Lake. It was about two miles wide, stretching eastward as far as the eye could see. The skies were clear, and it was savagely cold. Moving from the relative shelter of the forest, the steady wind from the north began to sting my face. I was relieved that it was only another twenty minutes till our sleds had turned onto Jon Bric's property on the south side of the lake.

He was standing outside his cabin to greet us as we pulled in, wearing a long animal fur coat hanging open despite the bitter cold. His thumbs were locked at the bottom of wide, red suspenders, which held up his loosely-fitted canvas trousers. He wore mukluks on his feet but no gloves or hat—a man entirely at home in the North Country. Jon's profile was pleasantly chiseled and manly, yet marred with the lines of one bereft of sleep. His naturally large, strong shoulders filled out his coat but were curiously bent over. These, I reasoned, were most likely the hallmarks of a life of manual labor.

"Welcome, gentlemen; I've been expecting you!" He gestured toward the smaller of the two cabins, perched on a small peninsula with two windows looking out on the vast reaches of Gunflint Lake.

"Our cabin boy, Devon Peters, just lit a fire and is stacking up a wood supply for you. It should be as warm as the Fourth of July within the hour." He laughed at his own humor. "Well, perhaps as warm as April around here! Meanwhile, please come in and warm up."

Bric gave us a short tour of the cabin. As we passed through the kitchen area, I saw a large bottle of laudanum on a countertop. I observed that it had not escaped the eye of Holmes either. While Bric was describing the intricate mason work on the fireplace, my mind began to turn over the reasons he might be using a powerful opiate, which could have been purchased at any apothecary. When speaking, he locked his thumbs on his suspenders near the waist. The fingers of his right hand were instinctively rubbing his belly and abdomen. He did not seem to be aware of this habit.

From the start, I was drawn to Bric and his rustic manner but hastened to hold myself to objectivity since he was a suspect in his missing partner's disappearance. Mr. Bric showed us into our cabin. Given the contrast to the massive red and white pines surrounding it, the building seemed almost puny. But once inside, however, it felt more spacious than I had imagined.

Holmes chatted amiably with Bric, asking questions about the local topography and his version of how the B & W mining empire came to be. I took a seat by the windows in a beautifully crafted chair made of diamond willow. Outside, I could see the silhouettes of Animikii and Sakima with their dog teams making their way northeast across Gunflint Lake toward their tepees. In a few minutes, the sky graduated from pink to magenta, then to deeper shades of blue, softly radiating out from the snow. The distant figures of the mushers and teams receded into the darkness.

Holmes finally came in and sat in a rocking chair near the fire. Devon followed him with a few armloads of firewood. Since Holmes was mute, I imposed a conversation on the boy, hoping to extract some useful information related to the disappearance of Mr. Karl Franz Weisner.

"Now, Devon, tell me any details you remember about Sunday, November 27th, when Mr. Weisner first went missing".

The boy seemed shy or embarrassed. He removed his gloves. Leaning with a hand on the fireplace mantel, he wore a blank expression and stammered as he spoke, "Well, sir, I came in early that day, say about 8 a.m., to feed slurry to the dogs. The previous day, Mr. Weisner had told me there would be no need to run the dogs the next day because he planned to mush them to Gunflint City for a business meeting. When I dropped by that morning, I fed the dogs and headed to the south end of the lake to feed and run Mr. Bric's team. Mr. Weisner never came out of his cabin, but I could see smoke curling out of the chimney, so I figured he was in there."

"Very good. How would you characterize your relationship with Mr. Weisner?"

"What do you mean, sir?"

"Well, did you get along well? Was he fair to you as an employer and landlord?"

The boy brightened a bit and flashed a quick, cherubic smile. Despite his long, unkempt black hair and bad posture, he was a handsome lad. The dimpled smile was perfectly framed in his mouth but spoiled by stained teeth that one would expect to be bright white at his age.

"Oh yes . . . both Mr. Weisner and Mr. Bric have been more than fair to me. I had no means of support after my mother died when I was fourteen. These men were kind to offer me a position. I am thankful for my good fortune."

I found myself saying, "It sounds like a great tragedy to endure for someone of your tender years," and then added, "How old are you now, my boy?"

"I'm eighteen this year." Devon looked back toward the door and added, "Well, I better get back to my duties, sir."

I looked to Holmes, who was attentive but said nothing. He just nodded to me, indicating that the interview was over.

After the boy departed, we boiled up some of the Madame's stew over a kerosene stove. There was fresh butter and bread as an accompaniment. The bracing outdoor air had keened my appetite. I felt warmth and nourishment reviving my body with each bite, yet, leaving me drowsy.

After dinner, we positioned ourselves in front of the roaring fireplace. Holmes loaded up his pipe with Turkish tobacco. He stood up and struck a match to the bowl with the bit clenched between his teeth.

Between puffs, he shared his thoughts: "At first glance, the evidence would seem stacked against Jon Bric. If not for the threatening note he wrote, we might speculate that Weisner died of heart failure, exposure, or a hundred other deaths this primitive land has to offer. The note only begs more questions: was it written in response to another message, presumably from his missing partner? And why would Bric incriminate himself by writing it in the first place? Why not just kill Weisner and make it look like an accident, thus reaping his partner's share? Indeed, if we are considering motives, then the bank investors should be suspect as well. For instance, the contract addendum gives the investors 100 percent of the profits if the partners fail to discharge their duties. If Bric landed in prison, the investors could claim both Weisner and Bric's stakes in the mine.

I guffawed at the idea. "Holmes, this seems a little farfetched." No response graced my comment. He picked up a few more logs from the carrier next to the fireplace and worked them into the fire grate with a poker. He then tapped some spent tobacco ashes into the fireplace and stood up.

"Watson, tomorrow we shall attempt to determine the fate of Karl Franz Weisner. Sakima, Animkii, and a team of our furred friends will be here at first light to help us begin our quest."

I saw my chance at an entire night's rest. Bidding Holmes a good evening, I climbed up a ladder into one of the two sleeping lofts near the roof's peak. A deep, plush bed of down and plenty of covers were waiting. I gratefully crawled under them. The creaking of the floorboards beneath me betrayed Holmes' pacing back and forth, as was his native habit. A heavy waft of freshly stoked pipe made its way into the loft. That pipe would be making itself one with the blast furnace of mind possessed by Sherlock Holmes, raging together in one great pyre of consciousness.

My own mind labored futilely at the mysterious disappearance and the prospect of finding a body in this vast, snowbound wilderness in the dead of winter. I drifted off to sleep for a few hours but was awakened by a series of booming sounds outside our cabin, strangely reminiscent of the sounds produced by humpbacked whales exhaling a blast of air from their great lungs. This memory harkened back from my days in the service when crossing the North Sea and made no logical sense. I might otherwise have risen to investigate, but the sound of Holmes' measured footsteps and the heavy scent of his tobacco told me there was sufficient vigilance that I might surrender to sleep.

Tuesday, December 13, 1892

"Watson! Watson!" A firm but gentle hand shook me awake. It was still dark, and it took a while before I was alert enough to recall where I was. I stared dumbly at the silhouette of Sherlock Holmes standing on the ladder that accessed the sleeping loft. He spoke sotto voice: "Our Ojibwe friends are here as promised. We have a long day ahead of us. There is a bowl of steel-cut oats and some strong coffee waiting for you, but we must make haste." I spurred myself into action, dressing, and eating. Sakima and Animikii sat in a stoic pose together in front of the fire. They declined Holmes' offer of food or beverage. Holmes was wearing the same clothes he had worn while pacing the floor the evening before. His face was haggard from lack of sleep. Still, his eyes shone. For him, the game was afoot, a reminder to me that he was never more alive than when the challenges to his powers were at their greatest.

Both native dog teams waited silently in the dark, harnessed to sleds facing north on Gunflint Lake. They turned their heads nonchalantly toward us as we approached. It seemed they knew the day's plan already. Being the only one perpetually befuddled in our collection of man and beast filled me with chagrin.

There was no wind blowing, but it was brutally cold. Holmes was engaged in a low-toned conversation with Sakima when the booming sound I had heard during the night repeated itself. My friend walked up beside me. He put his hand on my shoulder, and said, "Nothing to fear, Watson. You are hearing the sound of ice breaking under enormous pressure. This phenomenon happens in response to the cooling and warming of ice; it's a normal occurrence on the larger lakes in this area. I'll explain later."

"Holmes, are you sure it is safe to cross this lake? I can't think of a more horrible way to die than simultaneously drowning and freezing if our sleds break through!"

"I assure you, old friend, we are in the very best of hands."

With that, we took our respective places in the sleds and moved out from the deep woods onto the lake. I was now fully awake, awestruck by the heavenly vault. Beneath its population of stars, the puny people and their dogs were rendered insignificant. There was some light on the other side of the lake that I first took for dawn until I realized we were heading in a northerly direction. It was then that I realized we were witnessing an expanding display of the northern lights. It was as if a heavenly host held up a sheer curtain filled with cosmic-colored light. I pulled my hood off to behold the entire display, not caring if my head were to freeze solid. Of one thing I am certain: the memory of this will never leave me—the dogs running silently and the crunch of the snow beneath the runners while the starlight clock of the universe moved minutely overhead.

Near the middle of the lake, both teams stopped at a long mound of broken ice running east to west down the lake. We dismounted. While Sakima and Animikii walked and inspected the ice, Holmes explained, "My instinct to hire these two masters of the wilderness over their white counterparts is proving a wise investment. They are intimate with the nature that surrounds them. Sakima informed me that the sound of ice breaking at ridges is what awakened you last evening. The dynamics of expansion and contraction, especially between day and night temperatures can cause the ice to pile up at a weak point. In other cases, it will violently pull apart, issuing a booming sound. This often leaves a chasm of open water, such as the one where Karl Franz Weisner met his end. It doesn't take long for the open water to freeze over again in below-zero conditions. Most assuredly, we will take an abundance of caution when crossing over an ice pressure ridge, Watson."

The two Indians counseled Holmes. They had deemed it safe to cross at the two ice margins, emptied the sleds, and aided their dogs in moving them over the two-foot-high humps of broken ice chunks near where the break had refrozen. Sakima and Animkii walked alongside the sleds, preventing them from tipping until they were on a flat ice surface again. We mounted the sleds once more, moving toward the northern shore where the silhouetted treeline dipped down toward the cabin of Karl Franz Weisner—the last place he had last been seen alive.

Weisner's dogs greeted us with frenetic barking as we approached. Seventeen days had elapsed since their master's disappearance. The only human activity we knew of on the property was Devon Peter's reported daily feeding and exercising the dogs before returning them to their sheds. Due to the unknown status of Mr. Weisner, it didn't make sense to move the dogs, but the imperative for another solution was becoming evident. After consultation with Sakima, Holmes gave me a synopsis of our plans for the day. "I told Jon Bric that with the help of our Indian friends, we would feed the dogs and give them a healthy run. That will lighten the workload for Devon and give us some latitude to investigate the scene in privacy."

As the sun rose, the natives prepared slurry to feed the dogs. They removed the ten of them from their cages, feeding them and stroking their heavy fur coats. The dogs licked their faces, showing affection and whining, telling of their plight over the last several days. Sakima and Animikii made doglike sounds in agreement. When they were put back in their sheds, the dogs seemed content but watchful about what would happen next.

Holmes spent nearly an hour studying Weisner's damaged dogsled and then conversed with Sakima. Their hands continually gestured toward the lake. Later, I followed Holmes to a spot near the front of the cabin where he knelt, digging through layers of snow, peering at some brown spots a few inches under the blanket of white. Eventually, he focused his powers of perception on Weisner's cabin. There was no lock or hasp for a lock on the door; anyone could have meddled with any evidence that lay inside.

The structure was more of a lodge than a log cabin. Extensions spanned out from three sides rather than one conventional roofline. Diamond willow chairs and tables lent a well-appointed yet rustic feel to the interior. The morning sun poured in the windows, giving a false sense of interior warmth, for the temperature in the cabin was well below freezing. Our warm breath vaporized into clouds when we exhaled.

An indoor water pump was mounted next to a sink, a mark of luxury in the North Country. I tried to call Holmes's attention to it. He barely looked up, working methodically through Weisner's personal items. On the kitchen table, there was a pair of Weisner's glasses. He put them on, commenting that the owner was severely nearsighted. Moving to the bedroom, Holmes read through a pile of letters that lay on top of a dresser. He soon discovered a piece of evidence that Kingsley had missed: a photo taped to the bottom of a drawer. After a minute of close examination, he exclaimed, "Hullo," and re-read the letters. I sat in one of the chairs and waited for a directive. Holmes sat motionless for several minutes and then stood up abruptly.

"Watson, I believe we have turned a corner in this case; the next few hours will either bring us to a breakthrough or . . . a colossal failure on my part."

Contrary to his promise to the sheriff not to disturb evidence, he slipped some of the letters, along with the photo he found and one of Weisner's shirts, into a rucksack. Then he made his way out to the dog sleds. Sakima and his son were harnessing Weisner's dogs onto the damaged sled they had pulled without the benefit of their master on the day of his disappearance.

"Watson, what we are witnessing is quite singular: Sakima and his son can communicate with the dogs and extrapolate each dog's usual position in harness. From the dog's point of view, the musher shares control and sometimes competes with the lead dog for dominance. If you observe now, Sakima deduced the *lead* dog. It appears he also divined the *point* dogs and is getting the *swing* dogs into their usual positions." As he was saying this, one of the animals tried to leap over the dog next to them while they were both in harnesses. Holmes laughed and continued, "The dogs won't stand for their positions to be easily forfeited."

"Holmes, wherever did you get this knowledge? I've never heard you speak of sled dogs before."

"I borrowed a book on mushing from Jon Bric last evening. In addition to my contemplation of clues, I read the book at the expense of my night's sleep. During our mushing trip to Bric's property yesterday, Sakima told me he was confident that Weisner's dogs could bring us back to the spot he fell off or walked away from the sled the day he disappeared, so I thought it advisable to bone up on dogs and sledding. I am certain the case's resolution rests on the furry backs of man's best friends."

"This is incredible, Holmes," was all I could manage in reply.

We stood back while the natives communicated with Weisner's dogs. At Sakima's instruction, Holmes pulled Weisner's shirt out of the rucksack and let the lead dog sniff at it. Holmes grabbed a coal shovel that had been leaning against the cabin, put it on the sled in front of him, and then methodically lit his pipe. I took my place in Animikii's sled. The lead dog in Sakima's team looked to his musher for a command but received none. Man and dog exchanged eye contact for a few moments. The lead dog seemed to understand, tugging the tow line, and the team joined in. The sleds lurched forward onto the lake, heading southward.

The Gunflint Lake we were now crossing was markedly different than the one before dawn; the glare from the sun on the brilliant snow assaulted our eyes. The lake was over six miles long, providing a considerable "fetch" for the wind, creating miniature snow tornados that spun past us.

We were riding behind and to one side of Sakima's team. From that vantage point, I saw the determined profile of Sherlock Holmes, a pipe bit in a locked jaw, puffs of smoke swirling behind him. At an ice ridge near the middle of the lake, the two teams abruptly stopped. Several of the dogs were agitated and began whining. Their heads turned toward Sakima. He jumped off the sled, squatting by the lead dog, who barked sharply several times in a high and mournful pitch. Holmes stood up and walked to Sakima's side. Their hands gestured back and forth at a section of ice ridge that lay in front of us. The ridge continued from where we stood in both directions, bisecting the lake. Why did the dogs bring us to this particular spot? My first thought was perhaps their unerring instinct told them that crossing the ice ridge at this spot was unsafe, but I was wrong.

Sakima stooped down and released the head dog from the harness. The dog strutted back and forth and then laid down on the ice. He looked beseechingly into Sakima's face. For a moment, everything was still. I watched breathlessly. The native then pointed to the shovel. Holmes picked it up and began scooping the snow from one side of the ridge. He cleared a swath of some twenty feet within a few minutes. Sakima crawled on all fours over the ice, brushing the snow from it as he went, but apparently saw nothing out of the ordinary. Holmes had just begun clearing off another row when he stopped abruptly and looked downward, his eyes transfixed. Animikii and I made our way to the spot. Presently, our group stood at the clearing, peering down through the ice. A man's body lay prone, faceup, encased in ice. His eyes stared back at us, frozen in an eternal mask of horror. Sakima spoke in a low voice, "That is Weisner."

Part Two

Death, Deception, and Dogsleds

Holmes extracted a compass from his pocket, picked out two natural formations on the surrounding shorelines, then scribbled a note with their compass headings. Using basic compass orienteering techniques, he could return to this spot with relative accuracy. He shoveled some snow over the ice we had uncovered, addressing us in a dark voice: "Come, gentlemen, let us make haste to Gunflint City and report these gruesome findings to Sheriff Bowman."

Within the hour, we were standing in the jailhouse. Sakima and Animikii waited outside. The Pinkerton detective, Amos Kingsley, was there, a cup of coffee in hand. Our producing a corpse seemed to please him somehow. I felt my instinctual distaste for the man rise, but moved to the other side of the room to avoid the impulse to strike him.

Sheriff Bowman made hard eye contact with each of us and said, "None of you is to breathe a word about this until I say so." Each of us nodded in assent. "Mr. Holmes, you tell those Indians out there the same thing." We agreed to meet the sheriff and Kingsley by the ice ridge at 9 a.m. the following day but did not give them the specific location of the body. We excused ourselves and went back outside. I saw Holmes making his way down the mud street of Gunflint City into a telegraph office.

We returned to our Gunflint Lake cabin again by way of dogsled just as heavy snow began to smother the region. Not long after we arrived, there came a knock on the door. It was Bric; he made his way in amid a swirling torrent of whiteness.

"Well, men, you are back early! How is the investigation going? I pray we are close to an answer!"

Holmes responded, "I can't impart any news at this time, but I promise that you will be one of the first to hear of any developments, Mr. Bric. By the way, do you have a spare pair of snowshoes I could use? I would love to take a jaunt in the freshly fallen snow!"

"Absolutely, Mr. Holmes. I'll bring a pair right over, but be careful out there."

"I assure you I will—and now, Watson, let us get some warm food in us."

We had picked up a few extra meals, including ham and pea soup, from the Hotel de Marguerite before our journey back to the cabin. Ravenous, I found myself slurping it up. My good friend methodically brought each spoonful to his mouth in a more pronounced and dignified manner than my own. His brow was slightly furrowed in deep thought.

Holmes did not invite me to join him on his snowshoeing "jaunt." I certainly didn't feel slighted, having not the least interest in going out into the beastly storm, but I was more than a bit intrigued as to what he hoped to gain by running headlong into its teeth. With no further words, he departed, compass in hand, for the balance of the afternoon and into the evening. When he finally returned, his trapper's outfit was coated in snow, his face red and eyebrows extended theatrically with frost.

"By God, Holmes, you look like Methuselah!" I exclaimed. "You must be half-frozen."

He threw down his hat and laughed heartily. "Au contraire, my good fellow, the exertion kept me warm, and the bracing air made me feel like a young lad again. It whetted my appetite as well. I hope you saved some dinner for me!"

As we ate, I found Holmes to be jovial for a change. He recounted a herd of caribou crossing one hundred yards before him, barely paying him any notice. He waxed on about the pristine beauty of a boreal forest flocked in snow—everything except for the case. Whenever I tried to steer him back, he brushed my efforts aside as if to ask, "Why sully the dinner with disheartening conversation?"

After our repast, Holmes crawled up into the sleeping loft with not so much as a "good night." By the light of a lantern and the gentle popping of the fireplace, I lowered myself into a creaky chair with my sole company, a book entitled *Habits of North American Carnivorous Mammals*.

Wednesday, December 14, 1892

The following morning, at nearly 8 a.m., Sakima and Animikii showed up with one their dog teams plus Weisner's team in harness. Packed in the one sled were some tools that Holmes had requested. We left immediately for the middle of Gunflint Lake, where the loathsome task of extracting a body from the ice awaited us. Fresh snow had obliterated our tracks from the day before. Homes never needed his compass to pinpoint the crime scene: confidently, Weisner's dogs, once again brought us to the location.

Presently, two sleds appeared from the distant west shore and progressed steadily toward us. Kingsley, Sheriff Bowman, and an assistant soon stood beside us, looking down at the frozen face encased in ice. It took a surprisingly short time to extract the body with the ice saws they brought with them, for the body was only about four inches from the surface. Sakima explained the reason to Holmes: at the pressure ridge, an eighteen-inch gap of water separated the four-inch top layer of ice from the shelf of ice under it—enough space between the layers to trap a body. The ice on the rest of the lake was a solid block twenty-six inches thick. I felt providence to be on our side; otherwise, the body would have sunk to the bottom of this two-hundred-foot-deep lake.

With ropes and gaffing hooks, we managed to get the body out of the ice hole and into a waiting cargo space on the sheriff's dog sled. I summoned my courage, letting my eyes fall on the corpse. Weisner was dressed in a musher's outfit, gloves still on his hands. The sheriff extracted a sodden hat from the ice hole. Bowman then mercifully pulled a white sheet over the frozen face.

The sheriff looked down into the ice hole one last time and shook his head. He then mushed the corpse-laden sled into action, and the assistant drove the second sled bearing the shivering Amos G. Kingsley beneath a layer of blankets.

Holmes and the two natives widened the hole in the top layer of ice. He began working the gaffing hook with his bare hands inside the eighteen-inch gap between the two layers of ice. Soon his arms and hands turned blue from exposure, but he soldiered on. Eventually, two additional items were retrieved from the ice shelf: a left-handed mushing glove and a pistol.

Holmes sat back and put his frozen hands into his own gloves, wincing in pain. I picked up the pistol and saw the initials "JB" inscribed into the grip. "Jon Bric!" I exclaimed.

"Yes, Watson, Jon Bric," Holmes said in a dry and resolute voice. "That is an English-made Hopkins sixty-caliber dueling pistol, a percussion cap, muzzle-loading dueling pistol. It is one of a set. We must waste not a moment getting back to Gunflint City."

Within forty minutes, we were standing in the middle of town. Holmes turned to me with crisply spoken instructions: "Tell no one what we found until I return." He hastened once again to the telegraph office. When he returned twenty-five minutes later, he picked up the left-handed musher's glove we had retrieved and talked to Sakima for a few moments.

We then brought the pistol and musher's glove into the back room of the jail, where we found Kingsley and Sheriff Bowman standing over Weisner's body. With all the top layers of clothing removed, a gaping hole was exposed in his chest. Their heads turned uniformly toward the two objects Holmes held out in his hands.

Holmes presented the dueling pistol to Kingsley. "Gentlemen, in front of you lies some evidence that ostensibly points to Mr. Jon Bric's involvement in what we must now recognize as a most gruesome murder. However, it's not conclusive. Judiciousness demands that we now devote our time to reviewing all possibilities. Remember that the circumstances of this case involve more than one man's fate. There are millions of dollars in speculative investment at stake. There is no sense in causing a panic by acting in haste. Please note that the victim was wearing both of his gloves. However, I found this extra glove nearby in the water. It may shed some light on the case."

The lips of Amos Kingsley formed a snarl. "Mr. Sherlock Holmes, we thank you for recovering the gun and glove, which means we have sufficient evidence for an arrest: Bric's weapon, Bric's threat of death, and Bric's considerable monetary gain on one side of the equation. On the other side, we have nothing tangible against *any* other suspect. It would be an abrogation of our duties to allow Mr. Bric to flee from justice while we dither over surplus clues. We'll find their meaning when we extract a confession from him.

Holmes stood over Kingsley and said, "You're a bit too full of yourself, too eager to get the $2000 reward. Let me make it easy for you. If you wish to arrest Bric in haste, you can take full credit for doing so. If you're proven right, you will get the reward money. I will stick to methodology until a defensible conclusion can be reached."

Kingsley stood up eye-to-eye with Holmes for several long seconds, neither yielding. Sheriff Bowman squeezed himself between the two men declaring, "There won't be any rough-housing here unless you both want to end up in there." He pointed to the primitive jail cells. "Mr. Holmes, please pursue any lines of investigation you wish, but unless something drastic changes my mind, I'm inclined to arrest. What happens to the whole mining enterprise is secondary to the rule of law."

"That is a noble sentiment, sir," Holmes replied. "With your permission, I would like to take the musher's glove that I retrieved to aid in further investigation. I promise to return it tomorrow."

"You have my permission, Mr. Holmes. Oh, yes, Doctor Watson, I would like you to examine the body and give us your findings. Make sure that you extract the spent slug from Mr. Weisner's chest as well."

It was more an order than a request. Nevertheless, I went to work, extracting a typical round lead ball formed in a bullet mold. Someone with knowledge of muzzle-loading pistols had loaded the gun. Upon impact with Weisner's chest, one side of the bullet was smashed, but the other side was still round. We checked its circumference against the pistol muzzle. It fit perfectly. The pistol had been fired at close range to Weisner, as evidenced by the powder burns on his coat and the outsized wound. The impact could have blown the man clear off of his feet!

Our native friends and dog teams brought us back to our cabin at midday. Holmes nonchalantly informed me that he would return near dinnertime. The three of them mushed off once again toward the northwest end of Gunflint Lake.

I could have used some company during that time, but Jon

Bric, the chief suspect, was the only person available. I wasn't inclined to stop by for a chat but kept a close watch on his cabin and my revolver nearby. The only movement I witnessed was a solemn stream of woodsmoke coiling from his chimney.

Our usual dinnertime in the States had been six o'clock. I became concerned when two extra hours had elapsed. Finally, a few minutes after eight, I heard a dogsled pulling up outside. Holmes came in with the left musher's glove in hand and laid it near the fire.

I queried for more information over another meal of stew and buttered bread. "Tell me if I am wrong, Holmes, but you must have been on a mission to find the owner of that left-handed glove."

"Quite so, Watson."

"Then, did you meet with success?"

"Not conclusively. The glove may incriminate a murderer, but more interestingly, the pistol plus the glove may prove there was collusion in the crime."

"Collusion, Holmes?"

"Yes, that, or, at a minimum, the aiding and abetting of a criminal act. I suspect tomorrow or the next day, the final piece of the puzzle will fall into place. But for now, all talk is idle speculation. Now, I wonder where I left my pipe."

He got up and searched in his satchel for it.

Thursday, December 15, 1892

We woke early on Thursday, December 15th, knowing the sheriff would soon arrest Jon Bric. I looked once again at the smoke issuing from his chimney. He would be sitting inside, assuming the game was playing out. The end would not bode well for him.

Sakima and Animikii showed up with their dogs shortly before 9 a.m. Holmes bade them inside, where they waited by the fire. At Holmes' instruction, we packed our bags, knowing we would soon again be guests at the Hotel de Marguerite.

Within a quarter hour, we heard the approach of several dog sleds. Sheriff Bowman was in the lead, followed closely by two men, presumably deputies. Behind them was a sled bearing Kingsley, wearing his official Pinkerton hat. We stepped outside our cabin to witness the arrest.

Bowman pounded on Bric's door. It opened, and Bric stepped outside, dressed in cold weather gear and carrying a bag as if he knew he would be traveling.

"Mr. Jon Bric, I'm here to arrest you on suspicion of the

murder of Karl Franz Weisner. Will you come along peacefully?"

Bric showed no surprise, anger, or resistance. Curiously, he stated, "I've been expecting you, and I'm not going to make a scene, so let's get this over with." Bowman gestured woodenly to the empty cargo space in his sled, and Bric sat down in it, clutching his bag. The sheriff must have been grateful there was no struggle; after all, Bric was one of his benefactors. There would have been no mine or Gunflint City to protect without him. Surely, it would have been hard to put handcuffs on such a man. The solemn caravan of dog sleds turned onto the frozen lake, headed for Gunflint City. As suggested by Holmes, the sheriff and Jon Bric would arrive before us and proceed straight to the jailhouse so that nothing would seem out of the ordinary to the dozens of nearby B & W Mines employees. Meanwhile, Holmes searched Mr. Bric's cabin and quickly produced the mate to the dueling pistol used in the murder inside its wooden carrying case. It was in plain sight on the fireplace mantel. This, like Brics's air of resignation, further confused me. It was as if he wanted to be caught.

When we arrived in Gunflint City, Holmes made a straight line for the telegraph office. When he emerged, he was of shuffling step and dour countenance. This told me things were not going well. This case, I mused again, was beneath the dignity of Sherlock Holmes. Further, a pip-squeak of a detective was poised to take the credit from him! Although the telling of the crime might be colorful, it seemed a common murder, if ever there was such a thing.

Shortly, Jon Bric cooperated by giving a confession without providing sordid details. Kingsley pressed him hard. "Was this note promising to kill your partner written by you?"

"Yes."

"And this gun, the murder weapon, is it your property?"

"Yes, it is."

"Then you made good on your promise to kill him, did you not?"

"Again, yes . . . so why don't you hang me if that's what you're going to do?"

John Bric said nothing more but began sobbing into his hands. We left jail and returned to Sakima and his son.

After extracting our bags from the sleds, Holmes dispatched the two on a mission. I watched them disappear over a rise and up into the vast forest.

Two well-dressed men stepped off the train at noon and walked posthaste toward the jail. I learned that the railroad line was not officially open to the public yet, but anyone with connections, which these two apparently had, could wheedle a free ride before the inaugural run in January.

One of the men had a camera and tripod in tow. Holmes looked over at them and grumbled. "Watson, in my pursuit of evidence, I'm afraid I put the hounds of the press on our trail."

He had forecasted accurately. While we dined at the hotel, they entered the door and approached our table.

"Mr. Sherlock Holmes, I presume," said one, removing his hat and bowing slightly. "My name is Arnold Peltier. I'm a reporter for the *Duluth News Tribune*." He gestured to his companion. "This is my photographer, Jack Burns. Our editor, Spencer Dupont, informed us there was some breaking news in the disappearance of Karl Weisner, and we're here to get the story. We've noticed that something is going on at the jail, but we have been refused entry. What can *you* tell us?"

Holmes replied, "When I wired Mr. Dupont, he promised to do some research in return for an exclusive story, but *after* we have completed our investigation. We will get back to you when we have done so."

"Well, Mr. Holmes, I understand Mr. Dupont has several

people working on your request, and he will wire you as soon as he finds whatever he is after, but meanwhile, I think the public has the right to know any developments you may have."

Holmes told them no more. Undeterred, they rented a hotel room from the Madame and soon sat strategically at a window with a clear view toward the jailhouse.

Holmes made a quick trip to the jail and pulled curtains across the windows.

Friday, December 16, 1892

The following day brought with it a conclusion to the whole affair in a most spectacular manner, thanks to the persistence of Sherlock Holmes: At 9 a.m., he emerged triumphant from the telegraph office. He crossed the frozen mud street and entered the jailhouse, where I waited. Momentarily pulling a window curtain aside, he whispered under his breath, "Watson, the pieces of the puzzle are fitting together. We just need the presence of one key player, who approaches now." The lone figure of Devon Peters, wearing a pair of snowshoes, approached the jail entrance. Sheriff Howard Bowman opened the door and bade Devon step inside for a conversation. The two newspapermen has noticed this and were soon loitering in the street, waiting for any crumb of a story.

Devon removed his snowshoes and stepped into the jailhouse with trepidation. Holmes, Amos Kingsley, Jon Bric, and I watched him intently.

"Thanks for making the trip here, Devon. Please sit down, son," the sheriff intoned, indicating an empty chair. "Mister

Sherlock Holmes, with whom you are acquainted, has some questions regarding the disappearance of Karl Weisner. Well, perhaps I should correct myself because Mr. Weisner is no longer missing."

"Then you've found him, sir?"

"More than that, Devon: we've found him brutally murdered."

"Oh, holy saints, that is most tra-tragic, sir!" the boy stuttered, looking down at the rough-hewn floor.

Holmes broke in, "With your kind permission, Sheriff Bowman, may I conduct this interview?"

"Go ahead, Mr. Holmes; it's your party."

Holmes began his cross-examination with a statement. "B & W Mines was excessively generous in giving you an easy job with a beautiful new cabin. This generosity struck me as unwarranted, especially when the vacant cabin near Mr. Bric's would have sufficed. When I was looking for evidence last Tuesday at the late Mr. Weisner's residence, I found this photo taped to the bottom of his bedroom drawer." Holmes produced a posed studio photo, a facial portrait of a beautiful woman. Her left hand cradled part of her head. She had the fetching, dimpled smile of a starlet. It was signed "All my Love, Arlene." Embossed on the back of the photo was the stamp of La Roche Studios.

"On Tuesday, December 13th, I wired La Roche Studios, asking if they had taken any photos in the 1870s of a strikingly lovely woman named Arlene. A reply came back from Mr. William La Roche, who is presently running the business. His father, Andre, who took the original picture, remembered the photo session well, estimating it probably took place in 1870. The subject was a local singer and actress named Arlene Foster. Andre had followed her budding career and was an ardent follower as well. A year or two later, he did another photo session intended to accompany the engagement announcement of Arlene and her fiancée. Andre didn't remember the man's name but thought he was a mining speculator.

Holmes looked to Devon and continued, "After I met you and subsequently found Arlene's photo in Mr. Weisner's cabin, I noted the physical similarities between her and you. I concluded that you two are perhaps related—most likely mother and son. The dimpled cheeks you share could be a coincidence, but the crook in Arlene's left little finger, a trait you carry, was the clincher for me."

Sheriff Bowman's face wore an incredulous expression. He picked up Devon's left hand to verify this and exclaimed, "So . . . this little bugger's family name is Foster, not Peters . . .is that it?"

Holmes nodded matter-of-factly and said, "It seems to be the case, is it not, Devon, that Arlene Foster is your mother?"

Devon replied guardedly, "Well, ok, yes, it's true, but I had my reasons for not using my real name . . . and where's the crime in that?"

Holmes continued, "That in itself is not a crime. However, Arlene's photograph led me to more information. I sent another wire to the *Duluth News Tribune* on Wednesday last and received a reply today. They discovered an 1872 engagement announcement between Miss Foster and the late *Mr. Weisner*, both of whom resided in Virginia, Minnesota, at the time."

Holmes turned to Mr. Bric. "I have reviewed the public records of B & W Mines and learned that you and Mr. Weisner had been partners since 1871. You worked and resided on the same premises in Virginia, Minnesota, in 1872. I made inquiries to the St. Louis County vital records office and found that Arlene Foster gave birth to Devon Foster in 1874 in the city of Duluth. There was no father's name included in the record." Holmes stopped speaking momentarily.

Neither Jon Bric nor Devon filled the void; they stared stonily at Holmes as the story unraveled.

"I asked myself, if Mr. Weisner was Devon's father, why would the boy need to be using an alias? Since his family name was Foster and not Weisner, there was no ostensible reason for maintaining a false identity to avoid a scandal, at least as far as the public was concerned. But it would be imperative to keep Devon's real identity from his mother's jilted fiancée, would it not, Mr. Bric?

Jon Bric began quivering and spoke between sobs, "You are a clever man, Mr. Holmes—yes, you know it, and soon the world will know. Devon is my son. In Virginia, while Karl was away on business, I became romantically involved with Arlene. It was a betrayal of my partnership with Karl. I held a grudge against him for intimidating me into taking a smaller share in our partnership due to his being more literate than I. But I found I could prevail in the game of love and choose to act with dishonor. Becoming involved with Arlene was to risk financial suicide, but such a deep passion for her possessed me that I let myself fall into the abyss. When she became pregnant with Devon, there became an imperative. She broke off the engagement with Karl on the grounds that she stopped loving him and returned to Duluth, refusing all of Karl's entreaties to see her. He was devastated. In my cowardly way, I stood by, witnessing his grief, but I never confessed that I was the scoundrel who stole his love. Had he known, it would have instantly ended our financial partnership."

Bric finished the sad soliloquy, "I still maintained correspondence with Arlene from my location in Virginia and provided her ample income from that time forward. We tried but failed to maintain our intimacy over a long distance, but we always kept our friendship and our terrible secret from Karl during these many years. As horrible as the arrangement was, the profits from mining speculation provided Arlene, Devon, and myself with a comfortable living. When Arlene was dying in 1887, she told Devon the whole story about her failed engagement with Karl and it was I, not Karl, who was his father. I received a letter from her at the time informing me that Devon had been told the truth. Soon after her death, Devon showed up here with all his belongings. I told him I would try to be a father to him, but our lives would be far easier if we kept the truth from Karl, which resulted in Devon using a false name. From that time on, Mr. Holmes, I've been a nervous wreck."

Amos Kingsley had been listening intently to the proceedings. He couldn't resist his chance to induce Jon Bric into a full confession. "And you couldn't take it anymore, so you threatened Mr. Weisner and then made good by murdering him in your foul and cowardly way."

Jon Bric looked at Devon, who seemed frozen to his chair, betraying no emotion.

Bric said, "My son, let me do the talking now." He turned to Kingsley and Sheriff Bowman. "I am confessing to the murder of Karl Franz Weisner. I am ready to face the consequences."

Kingsley looked to be entirely satisfied with this confession but was chastened when Holmes stood up and said, "Sheriff Bowman, you are duty bound by oath to uphold the law and see that justice is served. Is this not true?"

His reply was gruff. "Of course I am, Mr. Holmes. Exactly what are you getting at?"

"I am happy to explain, but I need to discuss this with you privately."

"Very well, let's talk in the back room. Mr. Kingsley, please keep our prisoner secure."

Kingsley drew out his revolver, setting it on the desk beside his right hand.

Though uninvited, I followed Holmes and Bowman into the back room, grateful to find that Weisner's corpse had been removed. Holmes whispered to the sheriff, "I want to interrogate Mr. Bric with Devon out of hearing range. Then I need to interrogate Devon with both of them present."

"I figure I owe you at least that much for your help in the case, Mr. Holmes."

While Holmes interviewed Mr. Bric, Amos Kingsley pocketed his pistol and escorted Devon to B & W Mines headquarters, giving the two newshounds little information to chew on. According to the plan, Kingsley would accompany the boy back to the jail in thirty minutes.

With Sheriff Bowman present, Holmes began interrogating Jon Bric on the details of the murder. He gave a meandering account that contradicted the evidence Holmes had already divined. When he realized he had exposed himself, he stopped talking, but it was too late.

After the thirty minutes had elapsed, Kingsley brought Devon back in and sat the boy in a chair. Holmes bent over the boy. He casually filled his pipe, lit it, and spoke frankly.

"Devon, I think it is you who is responsible for the murder of Karl Franz Weisner."

Kingsley leaped to his feet, shouting, "See here, you pompous Englishman! We have a confession and copious evidence that Jon Bric did it! Now you want to intimidate a confession out of a boy to satisfy your conceit!"

The sheriff said tersely, "You shut your trap until Mr. Holmes is finished, or get out of here."

Kingsley snorted, then retook his chair. Devon's eyes shifted from one man to the next.

Holmes, nonplussed, continued, "Are you ready to admit to the crime?"

Devon's features hardened; the cherubic face changed. His dark eyes squinted with menace when he spoke. "Well, Mr. Holmes, I say . . . I did nothing. You're the one that's supposed to be so smart. Why don't you prove it otherwise."

"Very well, I shall endeavor to do so. From your father's statement, we know that you showed up in Gunflint City unbidden. I suggest that since that time, you have been extorting money and intimidating him into arranging for a new cabin to be built for you in return for withholding your true identity from Mr. Weisner. Your father must have told you he intended to name you in his will and perhaps suggested you would inherit his share of the mining profits in exchange for your silence. He may also have told you that he is suffering from a serious illness. The two bottles of laudanum, a powerful pain remedy, on his kitchen counter indicate that he is medicating himself. I have repeatedly witnessed him unconsciously rubbing a spot near his stomach. I infer Mr. Bric has a severe abdominal disorder."

All eyes in the room turned to Jon Bric. His mouth was an open expression of surprise. Still, he said nothing, waiting to see where this clairvoyant detective's recitation would take him.

Holmes turned back to Devon. "On the evening of the murder, you either told Mr. Weisner the whole story of betrayal by his sweetheart or he figured it out himself. It doesn't matter which happened; the outcome was the same. Weisner had discovered the web of deceit his partner had spun throughout the past nineteen years."

After a pause, Holmes continued, "The note Mr. Bric wrote to Weisner—'I will take grate pleasure in killing you!

Shister!!'—was in bold lettering and contained misspellings. It indicates that its author was an angry man who wrote hastily, in the heat of the moment. I believe it was in *reply* to a challenge issued by Mr. Weisner. I think that it was you, Devon, who delivered both notes via dogsled on Sunday, the 27th of November."

The boy and his father offered nothing in response to the brilliant monologue. The only sound in the room was Holmes striking a match to relight his pipe. "Mr. Bric, we found a pistol in the ice ridge near the body. In our interview today, you tried to incriminate yourself, but your recounting of the murder had little correspondence with what actually happened."

Holmes addressed the boy, "But you would be acquainted with the facts on a first-hand basis. I have deduced that the following happened on November 27th: Mr. Weisner somehow learned that you were the child of Arlene Foster and Jon Bric that day. He wrote a note challenging your father to a duel and ordered you to deliver it, which you did. Your father sent you back to deliver his threatening note along with a loaded pistol from his set, keeping its mate for himself in anticipation of a showdown. Perhaps as you were dogsledding back to Weisner's, you realized that if your father were killed, there would be no inheritance for you because no will had yet been written. You had to stop them from killing each other. But how?

"After you gave the loaded pistol and the note to Weisner, he was undoubtedly enraged. In the heat of the moment he would be intent on making haste to answer the challenge. Somehow his judgment was impaired enough that he forgot to put on his glasses. That would be tantamount to suicide in a duel-to-the-death, especially for someone as nearsighted as Mr. Weisner. Furthermore, we know Mr. Weisner was a very experienced outdoorsman, yet he drove his sled in a heavy snowstorm without eyeglasses into the water at an open ice ridge.

You had followed in his tracks with your dog team and saw his sled tip over on the ice ridge. The sled didn't go into the water, but Weisner was lying on the ice near the open hole. That was when you saw the opportunity to make his death look like an accident, wasn't it, Devon? But it didn't work out so smoothly. You tried pushing him into the water, but he resisted. You somehow got hold of his loaded pistol and shot him point-blank in the chest. Then you pushed his body into the water, anticipating it would sink. You then threw the weapon behind it, expecting that they both would find their way to the bottom of the lake."

Devon screamed into the face of Sherlock Holmes, "That's all very nice, but you haven't proven that I did it, Mr. Holmes!"

Holmes took a slow, thoughtful pull on his pipe and calmly blew the smoke back into the room.

"You are quite right, Devon. Nothing I have said so far proves that you murdered Mr. Weisner, but here is something that does." He took a rucksack from the table behind him and pulled out the musher's left glove he had found in the ice hole.

Devon's eyes grew large with fear, but he remained defiant. "What in blazes does that glove prove?"

Holmes replied, "The day after we found the body, my Ojibwe friend, Sakima was kind enough to mush me to the teepee of Namid, a member of his tribe. She told me she made these gloves for you a few years ago. She remembers the glove intimately: it was constructed of caribou hide rather than the usual moose or beaver hide, making it unique. You were probably pushing the body under the ice when your left musher's mitten came off your hand and ended up in the water, out of reach. You wrongly assumed that it would sink to the bottom of the lake along with the body and the pistol. Finding the left-handed glove created an imperative for me to find its mate. I made a trip to your cabin during a snowstorm the other evening, traveling by snowshoe, knowing that my tracks would soon be obliterated. I was pleased to find you were not home. My search revealed a half-empty bottle of laudanum on a countertop but, more importantly, the right-handed glove hidden in an outbuilding. Holmes then pulled the missing glove from his rucksack and handed it to the sheriff. "I am submitting this as evidence. Oh, one final item: The newer gloves you have been wearing since were purchased at the Gunflint City General Store within a day or two after the murder. The clerk has identified you as the person who bought them."

Devon looked up into the face of Sherlock Holmes spitefully. "I suppose you have me then, and I will pay the price for my deed! Yes, I did it! It happened very nearly the way you have described. Dad has been ill, as you have suggested. He has an aneurysm and expects to die when it bursts. He *had* promised to name me as his sole heir but never got around to making it legal. I guess he decided it was easier to keep my silence when he had something to hold over my head. Yes, Mr. Weisner finally discovered that Arlene Foster was my mother. He had stopped by my cabin unannounced on the day I shot him. I wasn't home, but he let himself in to warm by the fire; that's when he saw some photos and letters from my mother lying on the table. Mr. Weisner brazenly read those personal letters. In them, mom told me she was dying and that Jon Bric was my father. After Weisner read these, he was fit to be tied! As soon as I came through the door, he told me that the matter would be settled in a duel with my father. If Mr. Weisner prevailed, I was to pack my bags and never set foot in the region again. Before I left, he wrote the challenge, ordering me to deliver it to dad immediately.

Devon shook his head, apparently in disbelief that his own words could be true. "I mushed the note across the lake. Dad seemed as angry as Mr. Weisner. He read the note, threw it into the fire, and then sent me back with the reply note that you have there. He gave me one of the loaded pistols, ordering me to present it to Mr. Weisner and to return with the location they would meet in mortal combat. When I crossed the lake with Dad's reply, it was getting dark. I was half-crazed, caught in the middle of their standoff. When I got to Weisner's cabin, I gave him the pistol and Dad's reply to the challenge but told him I wanted to talk the situation over. He had been drinking. There was a half-empty bottle of whiskey sitting next to a full glass on the table. I was desperate and followed through with a desperate plan: I poured a high dose of laudanum into his glass from a vial I always keep in my coat pocket. That part worked; he emptied the glass of whiskey in one gulp before getting into his outdoor duds. I tried to stall him with my pleading, hoping he would succumb to the potion.

Devon's shaky hand waved in a gesture of futility as he finished his confession. "As we now know, Mr. Holmes, I was the wrong person to try to talk sense into Mr. Weisner. I thought the laudanum would sedate him, as it did to me when I took it for sport, but the combination of that and all the whiskey he drank made him go wild.

"Anticipating a showdown, he had kept his dogs in harnesses, ready for action. The next thing I knew, he had pocketed the pistol and stumbled into the yard without closing the cabin door. He scowled and yelled the dog team into action, disappearing into a blinding snowstorm. I looked to the table and saw what you observed, Mr. Holmes. Weisner was so intoxicated he had departed for a duel without his eyeglasses."

Jon Bric cried again into his hands. Devon's voice cracked in emotion as he continued his shocking confession. "I followed closely and let my dogs stalk his team. The dogs knew that Dad's cabin was the likely destination on the south side of the lake and could find it by instinct. Weisner's dogs also kept his sled moving straight toward Dad's cabin till they came to an open ice ridge and halted suddenly. My team was right behind them. Weisner tried to force the team to pull the sled over the ice ridge, but it turned on its side, spilling him out onto the ice. That's when I saw that his gun had fallen from his coat pocket. You see, Mr. Holmes, I realized one of them was going to die in a duel, and I wasn't going to let that person be my father. Then I thought if the authorities found Weisner drowned, it would look like an accident. I ran up and began rolling him toward the open water. He screamed and fought hard; that's when I grew desperate, grabbed his pistol, and fired. The force of the shot blew him backward into the water. Then, everything was quiet except for the howling of the wind. Even the dogs didn't make a sound. I stood there for a long time until what I had just done penetrated my consciousness—the horror of it! I was now a murderer and a desperado; my freedom would depend on ensuring the authorities never found the body.

"Yes, Mr. Holmes," he continued, "I did lose my left glove while pushing the body underwater and threw the pistol in the ice hole as well, figuring they would both sink to the bottom with the body. The darkness had set in by that time. I didn't know there was an ice shelf below the body, so I figured I was scot-free. I then led Weisner's team of dogs back near his property on the north shore. I wanted to make it look like an accident, so I tipped the sled on its side again and let the dogs pull it around the woods that way. My left hand was half-frozen as I drove my team like the dickens back to the warmth of my own cabin that terrible night. I never talked directly to Dad about the incident, even after the investigation began. I think he suspected I may have killed Mr. Weisner but figured the less said between us on the subject, the less we could incriminate each other."

Holmes then addressed Jon Bric. "Perhaps you thought it

noble to confess to a crime you didn't commit, making up for your absence while Devon grew up. You would be wrong on that assumption; Devon must come to terms with justice. We can only hope the courts will consider his youthful indiscretion and that he acted under the influence of a strong opioid."

The next scene was one of the most heart-rendering I can remember in my years of documenting the career of Sherlock Holmes. All was lost, and there did not seem to be a redeeming moral to the story. Weeping, the father and son held each other.

Amos Kingsley stormed out of the jailhouse and into the main street of Gunflint City, cursing the name of Sherlock Holmes. His voice faded with distance as he made his way toward a bootlegger's bottle store. He had inadvertently left the jailhouse door open, giving the photographer from the *Duluth News Tribune* occasion to document father and son in perhaps a last embrace before the gears of justice began to grind the remains of their lives to dust. Within an hour, the reporter, Arnold Peltier, had wired the story of the murder to their editor, but, as directed, gave Kingsley, not Holmes, the public credit for solving the crime.

My head was boiling from the senselessness of it all. Wanting to avoid all human contact, I slunk back into our room at the Hotel de Marguerite, not even partaking in dinner.

Saturday, December 17, 1892

I awoke the next day with the details of this nettlesome case whirling round in my head. We had uncovered more heinous crimes in previous investigations, but the perpetrators were clearly dedicated and diabolical criminals deserving of the rope. This crime was grave, but Devon Foster was still an adolescent.

There was enough dawn light in the window behind Holmes' bed for me to make out his silhouette: the sweptback hairline and long brow, from which extended a narrow, aesthetic nose. That nose was his indispensable tool: always the first in the room, the discerner of concoctions, nature, and perhaps even the scent of deceit. His head seemed as immobile as a Grecian bust. I didn't know if he was awake but ventured a try.

"Holmes?"

The lips of the bust came to life. "Yes, Watson, I am quite awake and have been well aware of your irregular breathing and restlessness the whole night through."

It didn't surprise me that he knew of my wakeful state.

What did impress me, and always has, was the singular, super-human brain, never idle. Even in sleep, it is whittling away at the indecipherable; always, it lives in a state of perpetual watchfulness. The room was quiet and void of distraction. The only stimulus was the pedantic yet soothing voice of Holmes.

"Watson, perhaps I can offer a mild elixir to help you sleep: I have taken some measures that will surely mitigate the excesses of the criminal justice system against young Devon. Yesterday evening, I met with the two bankers most invested in B & W Mines, as well as Sheriff Bowman, Amos Kingsley, and Mr. Jon Bric. They paid Kingsley and me generously for our services. I received the $2000 reward as stipulated. I gave Kingsley $200 of the reward money, asking him to do me the favor of publicly taking full credit for solving the crime, although railroad insiders and law enforcement know otherwise. Being in his cups, he suspected a hidden trick in the deal but couldn't reason as to what. He picked the money off the table with a guarded scowl. It was precious, Watson!" Holmes chuckled under his breath. I'm confident that Devon will receive a lesser charge of voluntary manslaughter—killing in the heat of passion. He'll need to serve a prison sentence, but it will likely be minimal considering his youth and being under the influence of a narcotic. The news of this lightened his father's heart a bit. I broached another sensitive subject with Mr. Bric: crime cannot pay. When Bric dies, Devon will not inherit his father's part. Bric understood and signed an irrevocable agreement stating such in exchange for a lighter sentence for his son. However, a trust will be set up for his legal defense and further education when he is set free. The rest of any inheritance with be given to charity."

"I feel better already, Holmes. Are we finished here and ready to bolt?"

"Yes, Watson. The partners have arranged for the train to

take us to Port Arthur. I wired Booth Fisheries. The *Hiram R. Dixon* is currently docked at their fishery on Isle Royale but will be notified to meet us when we arrive at Port Arthur. They will do their best to get us back to Duluth, but unfortunately, conditions have deteriorated on Lake Superior considerably since we first arrived. Near-gale-force winds and below-zero temperatures are creating havoc on the lake. There is another element, Watson: we must, by necessity, travel with the two reporters from the *Duluth News Tribune* and the intrepid Mr. Kingsley during the first two legs of our journey to St. Paul.

The only other option for travel would be to take dogsleds the entire distance to Duluth! But cheer up old friend; our journey should prove to be quite interesting!"

"Interesting, my foot!" I mumbled, half asleep. Holmes had eased my mind as promised. I gratefully yielded to a few more hours of rest.

We bid adieu to Madame and the staff at the Hotel de Marguerite, fortified by a hot breakfast. Holmes insisted we wear our trapper/Ojibwa outfits till our arrival in Duluth. The faithful Sakima and Animikii were there to wish us farewell. Holmes put his hand on each of their shoulders, reciting a tribute: "Without you and your amazing skill with dogs, I am certain justice would never have prevailed. I live in your debt."

Holmes used part of the reward money to create a sizable credit in the town general store for them, after which we boarded the train to Port Arthur. From our window seats, we watched Sakima and Animikii loading store provisions into their dogsleds. Then the train's shrill engine whistle split the frozen air. A cloud of smoke and water vapor from the engine plumed skyward as we began to rumble downslope toward Gunflint Lake and ultimately Port Arthur. I saw the frozen, rutted streets of Gunflint City recede as in a dream from which

I was grateful to awaken. The sky's strange pink hue was reflected in the snow. Thankfully, Amos Kingsley and the two newspapermen were in the next car. Intermittently a boisterous voice, which I presumed belonged to Kingsley, could be heard over the rumbling train.

Sunday, December 18, 1892

We overnighted in Port Arthur. By 8 a.m. the following morning, we were aboard the *Dixon* once again, motoring down the Kaminstiquia River into Lake Superior. An ice coating covered a solid inch of the deck. A northeast wind of 30 knots pushed us down the lake, but I was happy about this, for instead of taking the waves on the bow, we raced along and inside the troughs and gently over the crests. To our detriment, though, the shipwrights hadn't built this boat for winter weather; cold air leaked in everywhere. I was glad I had my Voyageur wool cocoon to see me through. At one point, I had occasion to visit the engine room, where, on the trip up the lake, I had previously sought warmth. There I found Kingsley by the boiler, shivering pathetically in his lightweight Pinkerton uniform and an equally inadequate wool coat punctuated with insignias on the collars. I allowed myself one verbal swipe at him. "Well, Kingsley, you look like you're dressed for a parade, and what would a parade be without a clown?"

We made two additional stops at small fishing villages

before dusk. The wind had died down. Clouds of icy fog encased the headlands, adding more rime ice to the boat's deck. The crew members obliged to be on deck, crawled on their hands and knees to avoid sliding overboard. A few sharp blasts of the horn brought rustic fishermen, seemingly of Norwegian descent, rowing their skiffs out of the fog to one side for unloading.

Both the port and starboard sides of the *Dixon* had cargo doors. One of them slid open when they arrived at a fishing village, and a boom would raise and lower the exchanged goods. The fishermen traded kegs of herring for various packages and provisions, including barrels of flour. I felt privileged to witness the wilderness spirit that helped to build this young country. In this case, the Booth Packing Company was aiding immigrants to gain a toehold in the New World, many of whom spoke not a word of English. The provisions they traded for would carry them through a long, isolated winter.

Pristine red and white pine forests came into view when the fog blew off. Incredibly, these magnificent trees were rooted in shallow soil, sitting atop formations of solid rock where they met the water's edge.

The captain gave a wide berth to the treacherous reefs beneath the waves. While I was in the engine room witnessing Kingsley in his misery, we passed the rocky shores of Mott Island. Two of the crew members operating the boiler recounted the loss of the SS *Algoma* in a late-season storm not long ago. "The boat was dashed to pieces with the loss of twenty-three souls," one of them intoned. This wasn't the kind of tale I needed to hear amid these treacherous reefs. I returned to my berth.

Monday, December 19, 1892

The night passed without incident. From my cabin window the following day, I watched the massive grey waters of Lake Superior narrow into the harbor towns of Duluth and Superior. We docked at about two o'clock on Monday afternoon. Holmes had holed himself up in his berth for the entire voyage but emerged looking cheerful and rested. We had both changed back into more civilized clothing and, upon docking, immediately caught a coach to an upscale hotel, dining and luxuriating as if we could make up for Gunflint City's privations in one day.

Tuesday, December 20, 1892

Holmes was awake early and had already perused the morning edition of the *Duluth News Tribune* as I took my breakfast.

"Well, Watson," he remarked, dropping the newspaper next to my plate of buttered toast, poached eggs, and bacon, "Mr. Kingsley has made good on his solemn promise to protect my anonymity."

The headline read, "Pinkerton Sleuth Solves Baffling Crime." Beneath this was a photo of the scoundrel feigning a gallant pose in his flimsy uniform. The obsequious story began, "The mystery of the missing principal partner of B & W Mines has been solved due to the persistence and acumen of one Amos G. Kingsley of the Pinkerton National Detective Agency. His astute instincts and powers of reason divined through a devious web of deceit and murder to finger a guilty party—"

Pushing the paper away, I exclaimed, "Holmes, I'm ready to put some distance between ourselves and that scallywag."

"There is a train departing for St. Paul at 9:45 a.m. I'm

loath to say, however, that we may still see or hear more than our fair share of Mr. Kingsley in the coming days due to St. Paul being the next stop on the way to his final destination of Chicago."

Still, my spirits rose upon boarding the train. The food was excellent, and the passenger cars were warm and comfortable. I prodded Holmes for more information about the case for my chronicles between snoozes.

"When did you first suspect young Devon of being involved?"

"When I met him shortly after arriving on Bric's property, I noted he had stained teeth. When I inspected Weisner's property, I found evidence of discharged tobacco in the snow. They were at different depths, indicating that someone with the habit of chewing tobacco had visited the property several times after the crime. I expected to find these stains only near the dog kennels, but they permeated the area as if someone were casing the property. Since we had the luxury of a limited number of suspects, my suspicions tipped toward Devon. In a short sequence, I found that Weisner had left his glasses behind when he intended to duel with Mr. Bric. Then there was the photo of Arlene Foster taped to the bottom of Weisner's drawer. As I have said, her dimples and the crook in her left little finger were manifest in her son. I began to suspect a cover-up maintained by the woman, Weisner, and Devon but lacked enlightenment as to a plausible motive. I soon became certain that nefarious intention was likely in Weisner's disappearance. Well, you know the rest, Watson."

"Yes, I do. It makes me sad to see how it destroyed everyone involved." Holmes considered this for a moment, then spoke as he looked out to the trees and countryside that rushed rushing by the window. "Be assured that you will find evil, my dear fellow, wherever you find the prospect of immense wealth. It is always there, and exponentially so in the vicinity of raw minerals and precious metals. Consider the scourge mining causes to the earth itself and the pollution it creates. When certain iron sulfides mix with air and water, they form sulfuric acid. The mining of it produces sulfuric acid when it comes into contact with water and air. As you know from your chemistry, sulfuric acid is hostile to organic life, and poor mining practices will result in polluted earth and water. By my word, Watson, human greed will make this happen on a colossal scale someday—unless our better side can prevail."

"Well, Holmes, perhaps goodness *will* prevail. After all, the greater part of the human race *is* good at heart. We also have extraordinary people like Sherlock Holmes who manage to get us out of the muck from time to time! I feel it's providential."

Holmes weighed this, nodding his head. I wasn't sure whether he concurred with my thinking or simply acknowledged the compliment. It didn't matter; I would quit the subject while I was ahead.

The steam engine faithfully pulled the train through the winter twilight toward St. Paul. Heavy snow began to fall as we neared the city. The prairie was deep asleep under the blanket of white. Here and there, a farmhouse came into view with a friendly yellow light spilling from the windows. I wondered what the people inside were thinking. What would they be doing a week before Christmas? Perhaps making pudding and crafting presents for each other, or maybe singing a carol around the warmth of the stove? This thought lightened my heart. By the time we pulled into the Union Depot, I felt like a character in a Dickens story.

We spent several days of leisure in St. Paul. The *St. Paul Dispatch* ran a front-page story with the banner "B & W Mines Murderer Behind Bars." It sang praises of Amos Kingsley, the genius who meted out justice. Kingsley had been greeted at the depot by a horde of reporters and the curious. He was the toast of the town, but it was consoling to know railroad and banking insiders knew the truth of the matter.

The railroad titan named James J. Hill arranged a banquet in Holmes' honor a few days before Christmas. His workers were nearing completion of a rail line that extended across the plains and mountain ranges from St. Paul to Seattle, Washington. Mr. Hill, enamored of Holmes' remarkable powers, offered him a senior security position in his railroad but was gently rebuffed. He conducted us on a tour of his seemingly endless Richardsonian mansion. A prominent musician treated the guests to a glorious concert of Bach's Toccata and Fugue in D Minor on the house organ featuring pipes that extended from the first floor up to a gallery.

We later dined in the most opulent room I have ever seen. Mr. Hill toasted Holmes several times. My friend received these accolades with equanimity. The evening was a fitting tribute to close one of the most trying cases in our many adventures.

Over the next few years, I inquired after the main characters in this mystery. Considering the gravity of the crime, I was relieved to find that the judiciary was lenient on Devon Foster. He received only a five-year prison term. Jon Bric died of an aneurysm within six months of our departure. Then came the Panic of 1893, which brought ruin to the investors who provided the financial backing for B & W Mines. For all the money and muscle that forged the railroad and opened the mining pits, only a single carload of iron ore ever rolled out of Gunflint City! The only enterprise that survived was the one purveyed by Madam Marguerite Matthews. I heard word that she set up shop at a logging camp in the wilds of Ontario, Canada, and continued to prosper.

Afterword

In the canon of Sherlock Holmes, the famous detective was never known to set foot in the United States. Yet, in keeping with his propensity to defy expectations, here he is! Indeed, several cases puzzled out by Doyle's Sherlock Holmes, including *A Study in Scarlet* and *The Valley of Fear*, include flashbacks set in the United States, but none where he set foot on its soil.

There is a period between Doyle's *The Adventure of the Final Problem* and *The Adventure of the Empty House* (1891–1894), where Holmes is presumed dead. It was during one of these years that *The Adventure of the Missing Partner* comes to pass.

The primordial isolation of Minnesota winters in the eighteenth century made it the perfect setting for Sherlock Holmes' foray into the New World. When I learned there was once a burgeoning mining company that fostered two boom towns, a narrative began forming in my mind.

The iron ore mine was served by the Port Arthur, Duluth and Western Railway, which stretched from what is now

Thunder Bay to the Gunflint Lake region. The whole enterprise went bankrupt after the Panic of 1893, with only one carload of iron ore ever being extracted. Sad endings can be the grist for good fiction, and it was doubly sweet to discover that this event coincided with the fictional gap in Doyle's canon.

There are conflicting historical accounts as to the exact location of Gunflint City, but the evidence seems to indicate it was north of the Paulson Mining Camp near Mining Lake but south of the Kekekabic Trail. There were a few buildings there, including a brothel named Hotel de Marguerite after the madam Margaret "Mag" Matthews.

I'm happy to report that the Northwoods still defy civilization. In winter, you can still stand on the southern shore of Gunflint Lake and witness the occasional musher and their sled dogs traversing through the blowing snow, eventually disappearing into the landscape.

Acknowledgments

I wish to express my gratitude to the people who lent their time and talents to help me hone this story from its inception to the completed manuscript. Reaching back, I must first give credit to a high school English teacher, Charlie Berg, who not only opened my eyes to great literature but gave me encouragement with my first short stories. My writing group at the Loft Literary Center gave me sage advice and support. All of my family members read and provided feedback, for which I am grateful. I want to thank my brother Charlie and nephew Jacques Charroy for their extensive reviews and editorial suggestions during the story's early inception. Brother-in-law Steve Irland lent his eagle eyes for detail in one of the later rewrites. A special thanks to Ann Possis of WTIP Radio and the staff at BookBaby for their proofreading. I am deeply indebted to Chris Wilson for lending his skills as an illustrator and designer to give the book cover its classic and fetching appeal, and to my brother Steve, who helped me develop the first concepts for that cover. Finally, I want to thank my lovely spouse, Gerri Barosso, for applying her scholarly energy to every aspect of the book. She sailed with me through the rigors of self-publication. Thanks to all of you for helping me bring a dream to fruition!

www.ingramcontent.com/pod-product-compliance
Lightning Source LLC
Chambersburg PA
CBHW010612310726
48969CB00010B/2672